Friendly The Fox!

Story and Pictures by
Ben Mann

Friendly the Fox

Was a gregarious guy,
With a sense of adventure
And a sparkling eye.

When he ventured about
He would always make friends...
In the forest, by the lake,
Where the *trail kinda*

bends.

But he helped her take *FLIGHT*,
He was that kind of fella.

But imagine his surprise
At the *kindness* offered back.

But he found him a leaf
And taught him to
sail.

But was offered a ride
To the end of the glade.

But don't you know Friendly
Helped her out with her
CHORES.

The friends that he made
Were from
all kinds of places.

All different **sizes,**

Diverse in their faces.

When Friendly was invited
For lunch by the tree,

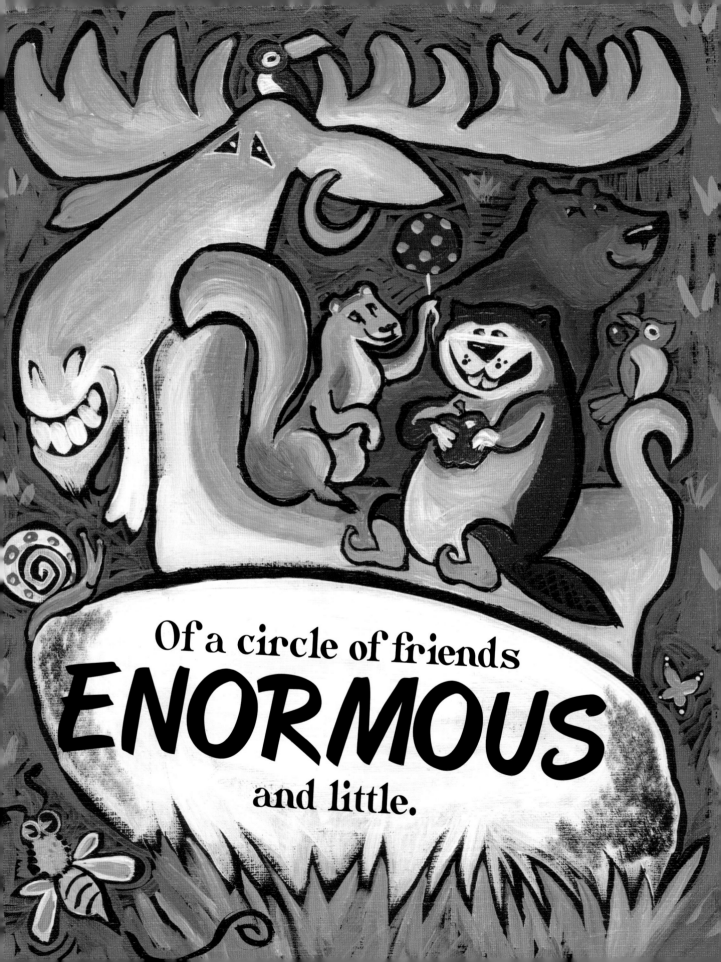

Of a circle of friends

ENORMOUS

and little.

That such different creatures Were happy and FREE.

Friendly dreamed that night
Of a Nature Parade,

You may find yourself
Having lunch with a bear!